BET 7.71

W9-ASL-562

ROTTEN ISLAND

WILLIAM STEIG

David R. Godine · *Publisher* · *Boston*

This revised edition
First published in 1984 by
David R. Godine, Publisher, Inc.
306 Dartmouth Street, Boston, Massachusetts 02116

Library of Congress Cataloging in Publication Data

Steig, William, 1907–
Rotten Island.

Reprint. Originally published: The bad island.
New York, Windmill Books, c1969.
Summary : Rotten Island has always been a paradise for
nasty creatures, until one awful day a beautiful flower
begins to grow, threatening to spoil the island forever.
[1. Fantasy] I. Title.
PZ7. S8177Bad 1984 [Fic] 84-4075
ISBN 0-87923-526-8

Previously published in somewhat different form
under the name of THE BAD ISLAND
by Windmill Books/Simon and Schuster in 1969.

Design by Jane Byers Bierhorst
First edition

Printed in the United States of America

There was once a very unbeautiful, very rocky, rotten island. It had acres of sharp gravel and volcanoes that belched fire and smoke, spewed hot lava, and spat poison arrows and double-headed toads.

The spiny, thorny, twisted plants that grew there had never a flower of any kind.

There was an earthquake an hour, black tornadoes, lightning sprees with racking thunder, squalls, cyclones, and dust storms.

At night it froze; all the living things stopped moving and turned to ice. But the volcanoes kept exploding, and the lightest breeze was a hurricane. At sunrise everything thawed out and moved again.

This rotten, horrible island was set in a boiling sea seething with serpents, sharp-clawed crabs, stingrays, electric eels of high voltage, and eerie fish with pointed

teeth, barbed fins and scales, and fluorescent lights that
glimmered in the bubbling deep.

The denizens of this sizzling-hot, freezing-cold, rocky, rotten island were monsters—huge or miserably stunted, fat or scraggly, dry or slimy, with scales, warts, pimples, tentacles, talons, fangs, extra arms, eyes, legs,

tails, and even heads, all in ridiculous arrangements. Some had armor-plating full of tacks and rusty nails, and some had wheels for legs. No two were ever alike.

The insects there could get as big as barracudas—
goggle-eyed with chopping mandibles, bug-eyed and
hairy, with stinging tails and clacking shells covered

with grit and petrified sauerkraut. There was no short-age of anything ugly.

All these horrid creatures dined on one another. The thorny plants were their vegetables; for dessert they had gravel. No one ever went hungry.

Whenever two of these hideous creatures passed each other, slithering, creeping, or crawling by, they'd hiss and spit and shoot a bit of flame by way of greeting.

They were vain and jealous. They could spend hours adoring their own ugliness, and resented any who seemed uglier.

Some lived inside the volcanoes. They liked to bathe in the lava, then cool off stretched out on hot embers in the broiling sun, dreaming up new ways to hurt, or planning how to get even for something that never happened.

Others liked to bathe in the sizzling sea, adding their poison to the water.

Nothing could make these monsters shake so hard with laughter as to see another one suffering pain.

They loved their rotten life. They loved hating and hissing at one another, taking revenge, tearing and breaking things, screaming, roaring, caterwauling,

venting their hideous feelings. It tickled them to be cruel and to give each other bad dreams. Rotten Island was their Paradise.

One day, out of nowhere, a mysterious object made its appearance—a lovely flower with blushing petals, growing in a bed of gravel. The first ones to see it were afraid, then very angry. They snorted fire and made menacing sounds. They had never seen anything so beautiful; they found it scary and repulsive.

Soon everyone heard about the flower and came to see it. And everyone was angry. They roared and hissed and clawed the ground. They wanted to be rid of that flower, but did not dare to touch it.

Another flower grew in another place, and then still another, at the foot of a volcano. The yellow gremlin who discovered this flower, a delicate pink posy, went out of his mind.

He ran raving over the rocks, howling curses, until he fell off a cliff and lay in a coma for two days, after which he got up and ran raving again.

The monsters grew more and more suspicious. They slunk about, depressed or delirious, accusing each other of planting the flowers out of spite, to spoil their paradise.

A hairy grapling decided to spy around at night and ferret out the culprit. He hid behind a rock and waited, but when night fell he was congealed into an ice statue, and never learned what he wanted to know.

The island was in an ever-increasing uproar. More flowers grew. More insults were hurled back and forth, more fire was spat. Their whole style of life was threatened and they were all dreadfully edgy, having conniption fits and nightmares—the kind even they did not enjoy. They were paralyzed with terror.

It got so the worst thing one monster could do to another was to push him into a flower. It made them hysterical with rage.

From cursing and blaming, scratching and shoving, they took to serious fighting, and all their deepest demons of hate tore loose. Much as they had all abomi-

nated and loathed one another before, it was nothing to how they loathed and abominated now. But it no longer gave them pleasure.

Battles raged. It was WAR! It was every rotten one for
his own rotten self against every rotten one else. Every
rotten one was equally furious and bit, clawed, spat fire

and deadly fumes, hurled rocks and burning lava, shrieked, bellowed, and screamed. They flung themselves one at the other, inflicting dreadful damage.

The sun burned hotter than ever, and when freezing
night came with its wild winds, the battle was frozen

solid until morning, when it thawed out and started all
over again.

It went on and on and on, and one day it was all over.
There was nothing left but smoke and smouldering
ashes.

Rain came, first pelting down in a deluge, then falling gently, a tender spray of droplets. It rained all through the night. There was no freeze.

At dawn the rain was over. And Rotten Island was no longer a rotten island. Where all those fearsome creatures had given up their ghosts, there were now flowers of all possible kinds, each one as lovely as the rest. The

ugly sea monsters had fled, leaving a clean blue sea. Over this flowering paradise the heavens were spanned by a glorious rainbow.

It wasn't long before the first birds came to the new, beautiful island.